This igloo book belongs to:

....

D0332451

igloobooks

Published in 2021
First published in the UK by Igloo Books Ltd
An imprint of Igloo Books Ltd
Cottage Farm, NN6 0BJ, UK
Owned by Bonnier Books
Sveavägen 56, Stockholm, Sweden
www.igloobooks.com

0221 004
4 6 8 10 9 7 5 3
ISBN 978-1-78905-656-3

Written by Stephanie Moss
Illustrated by Gail Yerrill

Cover designed by Lee Italiano & Justine Ablett
Interiors designed by Justine Ablett
Edited by Stephanie Moss

Printed and manufactured in China

Exactly
Like Me

igloobooks

My brown coat may not be stripy. I don't have spotty fur.
But when I **scurry** in the grass, I **whizz** by in a blur!

You won't ever find me with a sad, **grumpy** frown...

... even though I can't swing from branches or hang upside down.

I may not have a shiny horn or
ears that **flap** from side to side.

But when big feet come **stomping,**
it's nice and easy to hide!

or exceptionally **tall**.

I may not be **big** and **mighty**...

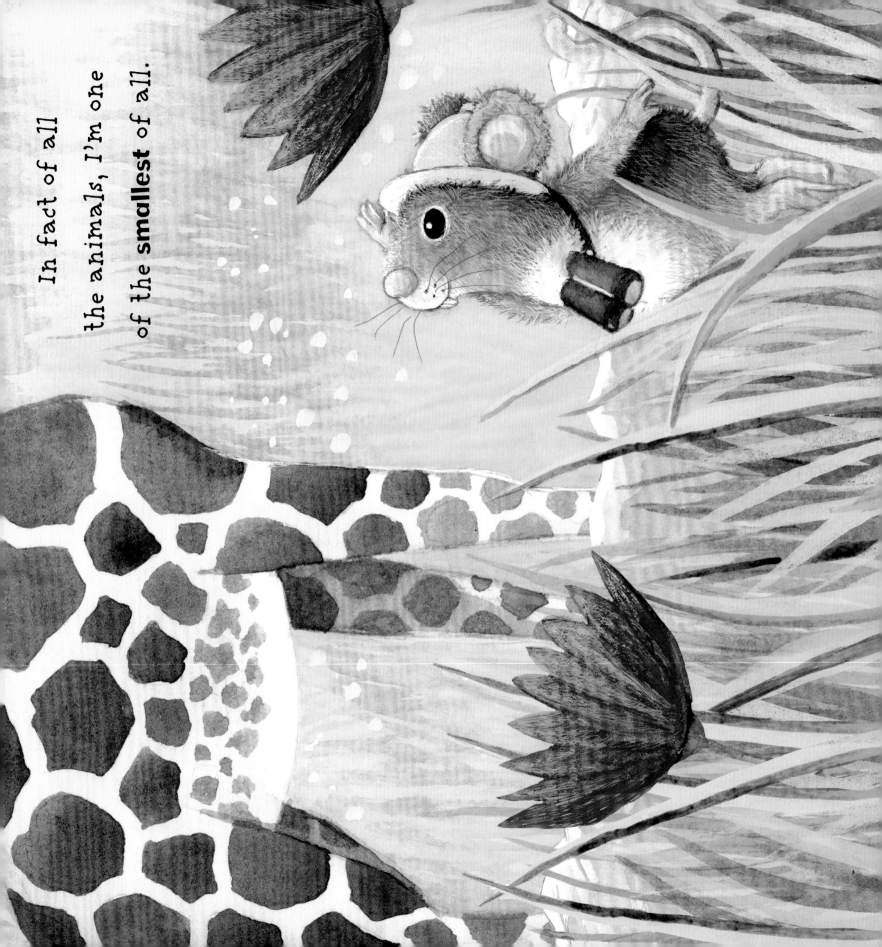

In fact of all
the animals, I'm one
of the **smallest** of all.

I don't slither or hiss. I can't **SNAP** with my jaw.
Though my front teeth are sharp, so I can nibble and gnaw.

You'll probably know me best
by my cute, little **SQUEAK**.

Though I don't have
pink feathers...

... or a bright,
shiny beak.

I can't **dive** into the ocean...

... or **slide** on the ice.

But most creatures that meet me think I'm pretty nice.

I love **wiggling** the long whiskers on my wet, shiny nose...

... so I don't mind going without wings
or a bottom that glows.

I can't see in the dark. I can't silently take flight.

But you can bet no one's more cosy when they're

snuggled up at night.

I'm not like any other animal in the land, sky, or sea.
But I'm perfectly happy being exactly like me.